A NIGHT OF *Lust* AND SEXTING

A Night of Lust and Sexting

Copyright © 2025 by Jennie Kew
Published by Wooden Key Press
Edited by Debbie Phillips
Cover design by Wooden Key Press

ISBN: 978-0-9756117-1-5

Size Doesn't Matter – Heart Award 2024
Erotic Romance – Winner

Size Doesn't Matter – Stiletto Award 2024
Erotic Romance – Winner

The Viking Blues – Heart Award 2021 (2022)
Erotic Romance – Winner

His Own Heaven – Passionate Plume Award 2021
BDSM Romance – Winner

This Time Around – Koru Award of Excellence
2020
Short Romance – 2nd Place

"Be prepared to be taken along on a
wonderful, sexy, heartwarming, sometimes
tear inducing, slightly kinky joy ride!"
Review for *Third Time Lucky*

"This novel was so romantic!
I'm in love, love, love with Rafe! I will
read this book again it was so good!"
Review for *This Time Around*

"It's a sexy, sleek and highly addictive story."
Review for *His Own Heaven*

"Their story is heartfelt, sweet, deliciously
hot and sexy, romantic and more."
Review for *The Viking Blues*

"It joins the rest of the series
on my keeper shelf."
Review for *Size Doesn't Matter*

"...funny and sexy, sassy and entertaining."
Review for *The Book Shop Girl
and The Billionaire*

"...very funny but also serious and heartfelt. "
Review for *The Roller Derby Darling
and The Delinquent*

"...unapologetically fun, messy,
romantic, and intense..."
Review for *The Drag Race Debutante
and The Detectives*

"I had a smile on my face from
the first word to the last!"
Review for *A Night of Lust and Sexting*

*For all the girls who like to be
ridden hard and put away wet.*

1

H*unter*

One of the things I appreciate most about my mystery girl is the fact she uses full words and proper punctuation when texting, as opposed to the often unintelligible world of acronyms and emojis society has come to accept as normal when communicating on our phones.

Mystery Girl: No shoes?

Me: No shoes.

Mystery Girl: Hot!

I chuckle as I type.

Me: Why is that hot?

I'm truly curious to know her answer and anxiously watch the little dots that appear on my screen as she types her reply.

Mystery Girl: I don't know, actually. It just is.

More dots...

Mystery Girl: I don't have a foot fetish or anything, in case you're wondering/concerned for my sanity.

I laugh out loud. My girl is funny.

Me: Good to know. Dare I ask what you're wearing?

Mystery Girl: Little black dress, stockings, heels, underwear that uses both science and magic to suck my stomach in to the point I might implode.

Frowning at my phone, I refrain from chastising her over her choice of uncomfortable underwear and type out the obvious question.

Me: Where are you right now?

The pause that falls between my question and her response feels like an eternity, but eventually the dots reappear.

Mystery Girl: Hiding in the bathroom from my truly awful date.

Me: You're on a date? Right now?

I'm not sure how I feel about this.
Pissed off is the first emotion that comes to mind.
Odd, considering I've never met the woman

on the other end of this conversation. I have no idea what she looks like or even what her name is. I have no claim on her, nor she on me, yet something doesn't sit right with me about this situation.

We'd started texting each other about two weeks ago when she'd drunk-texted my phone by mistake, then didn't believe me when I tried to tell her she had the wrong number. It was hands down the most entertaining conversation I've had in a long time. I'd expected the novelty to wear off quickly, but each message I've received from her since has only fuelled my curiosity.

And now she's texting me, asking me what I'm wearing, while in the middle of a date with another man.

I had no idea I could feel this possessive over a woman I've never met.

> Mystery Girl: Yes. And it's horrible. The guy is a pig. He keeps checking out other women in the restaurant, is a total narcissist, and he chews with his mouth open.

Mystery Girl: He also alluded to my generous size and insisted on ordering for me. A green salad, no dressing. Who eats salad without dressing?

Mystery Girl: Or bacon?

Mystery Girl: Or steak?

Mystery Girl: Or potatoes drowned in butter?

Ignoring the urge to smirk at her food rant, I re-read the first part of her text and my temper boils. Her date did fucking *what* to my girl? Taking a breath, I remind myself she's not really my girl.

Not yet, anyway.

Me: Sounds like a real charmer.

I will fucking end him.

Mystery Girl: I'm pretty sure I have parsley stuck in my teeth.

I smile again, her simple statement easing my tension a little.

Me: Do you need rescuing? Or dental floss?

Mystery Girl: Yes! To both!! But I'm a big girl. I can handle a bad date.

Me: Still, the offer stands. Just say the word and I can call you with an 'emergency'.

Mystery Girl: I appreciate that. But what kind of emergency would warrant walking out on a date?

Me: A family emergency, obviously. I could pretend to be your father or something.

Mystery Girl: Ooh, can I call you Daddy?

My cock twitches against my thigh and I have to shift in my chair to accommodate its sudden interest in the conversation. A lazy grin eases its way across my face.

Me: You can call me Daddy if I can call you Baby Girl.

Mystery Girl: Is it wrong that you're making me horny right now?

Mystery Girl: Do not make me horny when I'm on a date with an arsehole! I can't be held responsible if I do something stupid.

My grin dies a swift death and my possessive side snarls at her insinuation.

Me: Don't you fucking dare sleep with that prick. If I'm making you horny, then I'll be the one who takes care of you. Say 'Yes, Daddy' if you understand.

My dick is hard as rock and pushing against my jeans so incessantly that I have to let it out. The purr of the zipper blends with the ping of an incoming text.

Mystery Girl: Yes, Daddy.

Fuck. I want to wrap my hand around my cock, but I can't text one-handed. Shit. I'm so fucking horny right now. I want to meet this woman face to face, strip her naked and make her beg for my dick. I want to lick her pussy and make her moan, want to choke her on my cock and bathe her in my come. But she's on a date.

With someone else.

Not for long.

> Me: What restaurant are you at? I'll send a car for you.

The dots reappear, followed closely by an address and... fuck me. She's only two blocks away from my apartment building.

> Me: Baby Girl, go back to the table and await my call. Daddy's coming to rescue you.

2

E *den*

Oh, holy shit! The hottie I've been flirting with via text has just ramped up the sexy to eleven, and if I bite my lip any harder to contain the giddy squeeing noise trying to escape my throat, I'll make it bleed.

I straighten my dress and check my teeth in the mirror—no parsley, thank goodness—before leaving the bathroom. On the way back to the table—and the arsehole who thinks every woman in the restaurant wants to fuck him—I change the name I assigned to my mystery man from Secret Hottie to Daddy. I mean, I've never actually met the man, so I don't know if he's hot or not, but any man who can verbally spar the way this man can, and uses *their*, *they're* and *there* correctly, is hands down hot with a capital H.

And him calling me Baby Girl...?

Um... yes please!

I wasn't lying when I told him he was making me horny and wouldn't be held responsible for my actions.

Actually, I haven't lied to him about anything.

We've been texting for about two weeks, since my last first date went to shit. That guy had been an elitist academic twat who'd called me 'just a librarian' then proceeded to belittle my career, my life choices and the Dewey decimal system.

He also thought that because I was over thirty, overweight, and still single I'd be desperate for his cock, and since he'd paid for dinner, he somehow figured that meant he'd also paid for me. As if I'd give up the goods for the price of a steak and a glass of cheap wine. Arsehole.

Anyway, later that night in a drunken fit

of pique, I'd text-ranted at the fool for a good hour, schooling him on the proper etiquette of dating, getting more and more angry the more he denied me the satisfaction of an apology. It was only the next day while nursing a blinding hangover that I re-read the text exchange, double-checked the phone number I'd sent it to, and sent an apology of my own.

Daddy had been very forgiving of my phone-paux and told me I deserved better than the obvious morons I was dating. He also said some very nice things about the Dewey decimal system, and we've been texting ever since.

We don't share anything overly personal—no names, no pictures. And our flirting hasn't really been flirting, more of a disappointingly non-committal wordplay that skirts the edge of flirting without ever crossing that line. Tonight is the first time I took the leap and made that move. *What are you wearing?* A classic sexting opener.

As I take my seat at the table, my date barely looks up from his phone. "You took your time."

Forcing a smile, I say, "Yes, well, ladies bathrooms always have a line up." I pick up the dessert menu, knowing it will annoy him. "Mmm, this looks good."

The douchebag sitting opposite me lifts one brow and cocks his head in a superior fashion. "I'm not paying for that."

Just as I open my mouth to respond, my phone rings. My rescue is at hand. Keeping my cool at the thought of finally speaking to my mystery man is harder than I'd anticipated, but I manage it—just—and answer the call, noting my date's eye roll when I say, "Hello, Daddy."

"Fuck," he murmurs. "You have the sweetest voice, Baby Girl."

I swallow hard, trying desperately not to blush at the rich, growly voice invading my senses and making my panties even wetter than they already were.

Daddy sounds delicious.

"I'm on a date right now. Is everything okay?"

"You're on a date with another man who's treating you like garbage. Of course everything isn't okay."

I glance at my date again, but he's leering at the waitress leaning over the table beside ours. He's been blatantly ogling the poor girl every time she comes within spitting distance of our table. Her and every other pretty young thing in the restaurant. Narrowing my eyes, I say, "What do you need me to do?"

"My car will be out front in five minutes. Black sedan. Don't keep me waiting."

"Yes, Daddy."

The call ends and I grab my purse. Standing, I say, "I'm sorry but I have to go. My dad needs me. Family emergency." I don't even care that the excuse sounds exactly like what it is: an escape route.

Opening my purse, I pull out a fifty and lay it on the table. It's more than enough to cover the cost of the boring salad and shitty wine. As I pick up my phone, the arsehole sitting opposite me stares at me like he doesn't understand, as though a woman walking out on him—especially one who looks like me—has never happened before. And instead of lying and saying something about it being a lovely evening, or that it was nice meeting him, I simply say, "Goodbye," then turn and walk away.

Just as I push through the restaurant doors to the street beyond, a sleek black car with dark tinted windows rolls to a stop, and before the valet can even approach, the driver comes around the car and opens the rear door. Curiosity makes me peer inside where I find a drop-dead gorgeous, silver fox of a man grinning back at me, wearing jeans, a T-shirt and no shoes, with a phone in his hand.

My phone vibrates with an incoming text.

Daddy: Get in the car, Baby Girl.

3

H *unter*

The smile that decorates my girl's face when she reads my text is quick and broad, her dark eyes warm and full of joy. Her dress, stockings and heels accentuate her soft, voluptuous figure, and her lush, red lips make me crave a taste of her.

More than I already did.

She's a beautiful woman and deserves so much better than the fuckwits she's been dating. Insecure little boys trying to body shame and belittle her because they know they're not man enough to satisfy her appetites.

That's not a problem I have.

My driver takes her hand and helps her into the back seat of my sedan, and not for the first time tonight, an inexplicable feeling of possessiveness comes over me. I want to wrench her hand free from his. She's mine, and it doesn't matter how innocuous the touch was.

No one touches what's mine.

As she slides over the seat and settles in, I watch her assess her new surroundings, take in the polished wood and leather interior, the tinted windows that hide us from view. She taps out a message on her phone.

My phone dings.

Baby Girl: Thanks for the rescue.

I smirk and chuckle as I type my reply.

Me: Anytime. Now put your phone away and give Daddy a kiss.

She does as asked, slipping her phone inside her purse, then turns to face me. "Hello," she says, that sweet voice of hers sending a surge of lust directly to my dick.

How long has it been since I felt this kind of attraction, this intense need?

I need to be inside her.

I need to hear her scream my name when I make her come.

But I will control myself.

Even if that control is hanging by a thread.

"Get over here."

She wriggles closer, and as my driver pulls out into traffic, I haul my girl into my lap so she's straddling me, spreading her thick thighs wide over my straining cock. I say 'girl' but she is all woman. All soft curves and long limbs and heated glances.

Fuck. A man could tumble headfirst into love staring into those sultry bedroom eyes.

I slide my hand to her nape and fist it in the silky softness of her hair. The tiny gasp that escapes her parted lips is all the invitation I need to take that mouth and plunder it. She isn't shy about returning my kiss, her tongue a weapon she wields exceptionally well, and by the time she eases back and takes a breath, my cock is aching for her touch.

"Wow," she murmurs, her gaze glued to my

mouth. She traces the pad of her thumb over my bottom lip. "I had a hunch you'd be a good kisser, but... *damn.* You're amazing." She lifts that sultry stare to meet mine head on. "Do it again."

Laughter rumbles through me, her enthusiasm for my kisses puffing out my chest and flexing my cock. My so-hard-it-hurts cock. The urge to unzip my jeans and let it free, to take it in hand—or better yet, throw Baby Girl on the seat and plough into her juicy pussy—is driving me crazy. But I content myself with taking her mouth again and showing her with my tongue exactly what I intend to do to her with my cock.

A throat clearing from the front seat snaps me back to reality, and as I gently push my girl back, I feel the car rock as it enters the driveway to my apartment building car park.

"That was quick," she says, then looks out the windows on either side of us. "Where are we?"

"My place," I tell her, my lust making my voice drop low and husky. "Is that all right?"

She eyes me curiously for a moment, then pulls her phone out of her purse and takes a photo of me, and then one of my driver. "Address please." I tell her and she types it into her phone. A moment later she receives a text message and smiles, then puts her phone away again.

"All good?"

She nods. "All good. Just checking in with a friend in case you turn out to be a serial killer or something."

"Or an elitist academic twat who wouldn't know a good book if it smacked me in the face?" I joke, repeating one of the rants she'd texted at me the night we 'met'.

A burst of laughter explodes out of her. I like the sound. It's feminine yet robust. Free and unapologetic. "I'm so sorry about that," she says as my driver pulls into my designated parking space.

I fist my hand in her hair again and tug her closer, feel her soft flesh mould to my hard chest. "I'm not."

The need I see in her eyes, hear in the catch of her breath, is all the permission I need. I take her mouth again, wrestle her tongue into submission and revel in her moan and the way she fists her hands in my shirt, pulling me closer.

This woman is driving me crazy.

And I don't even know her name.

4

E *den*

I feel the car come to a stop and try to pull back from the best kiss of my life. Counterproductive, sure, because I absolutely do not want this feeling of utter bliss to end, but unless we're about to get it on in the back seat of his car, I'm seeing few other options.

When the back door pops open, I look up to see the driver grinning. When I catch his gaze, he winks at me, then holds out his hand.

I tug at my skirt in a vain attempt to cover

myself before exiting the car—the driver has had enough of a show without seeing my soaked panties, too—but as I reach towards him, I hear the word, "No", and as quick as lightning, Daddy has me laid out on the back seat, his heavy weight pressing me into the soft leather, his strong hands banded around my wrists. His thick, hard cock stabbing between my thighs.

Daddy rocks his hips against me and my eyelids flutter down, blocking out everything but the warm weight on top of me and the soft growl by my ear.

"Mine."

My eyes pop open and I stare into the intense blue gaze of the man above me. I don't even know his name—not his real name, anyway—but here I am, pinned down and panting, any sense of self-preservation but a distant memory, waiting to see what will happen next. No man has ever said that to me before.

Mine.

Like I'm his possession.

His vehemence sends a shiver through me, but I have to admit, I don't hate it as much as I thought I would. But maybe that has more to do with who said it than the meaning be-hind it.

"Finley."

"Hmm?"

"Take the rest of the night off."

Daddy's gaze doesn't leave mine as he speaks to his driver, and it's hard to ignore the sexy grin curling his lips. A deep chuckle sounds from outside the car, followed by, "You got it, boss. Enjoy your evening, miss."

"I'm sure I will," I purr, flexing my hips up-wards until I feel Daddy's hard length stab into me again. Another warm chuckle greets my ears before the car door is gently closed, and Daddy and I are completely alone.

At last.

And hey, I guess we *are* about to get it on in the back seat of his car.

"Baby Girl, you are so fucking beautiful. I can't believe I have you here, in my grasp."

I smile at his words, at the wonder I hear in his voice as he says them. "I can't believe you're even hotter in real life than you were in my imagination."

A devastating grin flashes across his face and his hands tighten around my wrists. "I was going to wait until I got you up to my penthouse before fucking you, but I can't wait that long. I want to be inside you." He pauses to stare at me. "Is that okay?"

Did he just ask if it was okay to have sex with me in the back of his car like a pair of horny teenagers? I can't help but push this boundary a little. Test what I'm up against. "And if I say no?"

He chuckles and lowers his forehead to mine. "Then I hope you enjoy having your pussy eaten in an elevator, because I need to taste you. Now. And I don't much care where we are." He flexes his hips, rubs his hard length against me and moans. "But since the elevator has cameras and the car doesn't, I thought you might be more comfortable in here."

Wow. Hot and thoughtful. Such a rare combination, in my experience. I narrow my gaze on his for a moment, then nod. "Okay. Car sex first, then pussy eating in the elevator."

Daddy laughs and the rich, genuine sound of it makes my belly do more backflips than an Olympic gymnast on speed. "Greedy girl. I like that."

My lips twist to one side as I debate sharing something with him. Mind made up, I glance away, my everyday awkwardness rising to the surface. "Truth be told, I never had many of the typical teen experiences growing up. Never got invited on a date. Never made out in the back seat of a car." I shrug, still avoiding his gaze. "I did get bullied, though. Didn't miss out on that experience."

I'm rambling now. I know I am. I'm screwing everything up. Any second now I'm going to feel that gorgeous cock grow soft and he'll realise what a colossal mistake he's made meeting me in person.

I am so much cooler on the other end of an anonymous text chain.

Suddenly Daddy grabs my chin in one hand and forces my gaze to his. "Look at me, Baby Girl. Stay with me. Fuck those memories. Fuck those kids who couldn't see your worth. Fuck that idiot you were out with tonight and every other shitty date you've been on. You're with me now, and we're going to make some new memories." He strokes my cheek. "I see your beauty." He kisses my lips. "I see your intelligence." He nuzzles against my neck. "I see you, sweet girl."

Now he's staring down at me like he wants to devour me whole and, I gotta say, I am one hundred per cent here for it, even if experience tells me his words don't ring quite true. Men who look like him don't say things like that to chicks who look like me.

Still, what little resistance I have dissolves and my legs part like the Pearly Gates. Daddy's hips sink further between my thighs and that rock-hard cock presses even harder against my clit. We both moan, and I think my eyes roll back. How long has it been since I had sex? Since I was well and truly fucked?

Too fucking long.

"Daddy?"

"Yes, Baby Girl?"

"Can we have sex now?"

That devilish grin of his is back. "Whatever you want, sweetheart."

In a flurry of action my stockings are ripped, and my wonder panties are yanked down my legs and discarded, and Daddy's jeans are torn open and sitting low on his hips, and if I ever thought condoms weren't sexy it's only because I have never seen a man take such care to roll one on so sensually it takes my breath away.

Holy prophylactic, Batman.

That was hot!

But not as hot as my lover's gaze as he

lowers himself over me again and guides himself inside me. I'm so eager for him, so horny, so wet, he slides in right to the hilt with ease.

"Fuck, Baby Girl." He groans. "You are so fucking tight." I can only moan in response. He presses into me, lays his weight on top of me. "So soft and hot. So wet," he murmurs against my neck. "Fucking beautiful."

And then he hooks one of my legs over the crook of his arm and opens me up to even more sensation. "Daddy," I moan. "Yes. Fuck, yes."

"Tell me your name," he whispers, his breathing ragged against my skin. "Your real name."

"Eden. My name is Eden."

Daddy stops moving and stares down at me, one brow cocked. "Seriously?" When I nod he laughs, but there's nothing mocking about it. He sounds... happy. As if he just learned something wonderful. "I'm having the best sex I've had in years with a woman whose name literally means paradise? Fuck me, if you aren't just the most perfect little thing, Baby Girl."

My mouth falls open and I blink up at him. Perfect and little are two words no one has *ever* used to describe me, at least not sincerely. But as he begins moving in me again, slowly rolling his hips so I feel every inch he has to give me, everywhere he wants to give it, a rush of warmth fills my heart as I realise he might actually mean it.

Mind. Blown.

Forget how long it's been since I had good sex. How long has it been since I wasn't treated as lesser than? How long since I wasn't an afterthought, or the butt of a joke, or a last resort?

"What's your real name?" I pant the words in his ear.

"Hunter."

Hunter. I guess that makes me his prey. "Fuck me, Hunter. Hard."

He cocks one brow. "Ask me nicely, Baby Girl."

His suddenly stern voice makes me shiver, makes me eager to obey. "Please fuck me hard, Daddy."

Without another word, he thrusts hard and deep, giving me exactly what I asked for. Exactly what I need. And it doesn't take long for my body to tighten in all the best places, for my brain to light up like a Roman candle, obliterating every other thought, every other feeling, until there is only me and Hunter and this feeling of total and utter abandon.

Complete, mind-altering bliss.

The aftermath is a blur of tugging clothes back into place, punctuated with giggling on my part, and little nibbles along my jaw and neck on his. But finally the car door pops open and we emerge into the shadowy underground car park, and I finally realise why he called me little.

Daddy is a *big* man. Bigger than I'd realised, curled into the back seat of his sedan. I mean, I'm considered tall most days of the week, and my stilettos push me over six feet, but Daddy—Hunter—towers over me. And when he takes my hand and leads me to the elevator a few metres away, threads our fingers together, lifts my hand to his lips and kisses it... I am en-thralled.

"You still want me to eat your pussy in there?" he says, his voice gravelled by lust, even as he grins down at me and nods towards the elevator.

I return his grin, my confidence buoyed by our afterglow from the car sex. "I'd hoped you were a man of your word,"—I shrug, trying to look innocent—"but if it's too much for you...."

"Oh, them's fightin' words, Baby Girl." The doors slide open. "Get your sexy arse inside and brace yourself." He slaps my butt as way of shoving me inside the small elevator. "And baby?"

"Hmm?"

"Don't forget to smile for the camera."

5

H*unter*

I lead Eden to the elevator and guide her inside, electricity sparking along my skin where our fingers intertwine. I need to touch her. To ground myself in the moment with her. To know she's real, she's here. She's mine.

Eden.

It's the perfect name for my girl. She is the embodiment of paradise, all long limbs and soft flesh, a wealth of curves wrapped in a sexy little dress and stilettos. Her stockings and magic underwear are gone. I ripped those off her the second she gave me her consent, revealing smooth, shapely calves and well-padded thighs.

The perfect cradle for my body.

I can't wait to get her upstairs and strip her naked, to see if the rest of her body flushes pink the way her cheeks do when she comes.

Don't even get me started on the sweet little noises she makes, or the way her mouth forms a perfect O as she makes them. Or the way her eyes squeeze shut, then blink open to stare up at me, lock on to me with laser focus and bore down to my very soul.

Fuck. My dick is getting hard again just thinking about that soul-stirring stare. Most people can't even bring themselves to look me in the eyes, let alone *stare* into them. I don't have the nicest reputation. In fact, in certain circles I'm a renowned arsehole to be avoided at all costs. Such is the life of a lawyer. Which makes Eden's directness a welcome change.

And I intend to reward her for it.

The elevator doors begin to close. I drop Eden's hand and swipe my key card for executive access to the penthouse, then shove it back in my pocket. Eden leans against the back wall of the elevator, her arms spread wide and her hands gripping the courtesy rail behind her, doing exactly what I told her to do.

She's bracing herself.

Waiting for me to eat her pussy in full view of the security camera and the pervert night-watchman in the security room. I'll have Finley erase the evidence later.

Stepping towards her, I cup her face, draw her to me and take her mouth, lick my way between her lips and devour her.

And there are those little noises again. Filling my head with devilish thoughts.

I'm glad the security camera is vision only, no sound, because I'm not sharing these noises, Eden's noises, with anyone.

They're mine, too.

I work my way over her chin and along her jaw, nuzzle into the sweet spot just below her ear. Down her neck to the hollow of her throat, then lower still, following the deep V of her neckline until my lips brush over the plump curve of her cleavage.

She shivers and sags against the railing. "Hunter."

Her voice is soft and pleading and I find I like hearing my name in that soft tone almost as much as I like her calling me Daddy.

I am such a dirty fucker.

The flick of her tongue across her lips draws my attention back to her face, back to those deep, dark eyes. Eyes filled with lust and promises.

Speaking of promises....

I run my hands down her sides, to where the hem of her dress wraps around her mid-thigh, grip the fabric and drag it north, expose those fleshy thighs to my hungry gaze once more. She gasps then bites her bottom lip. Her chest heaves with shortened breaths as I lower myself to my knees and shove her dress higher, bunch it around her waist, fully exposing her soft belly and freshly waxed mound.

I lick my lips. "Are you ready for me, Baby Girl?"

She nods, her lip slipping free from the grip of her teeth. "Yes, Daddy."

I nudge her legs further apart, press my face against her pussy and breathe her in. *Fuck.* She smells like sex and sweet feminine heat. So fucking good. "Hold on tight, baby," I murmur, then slip two fingers deep inside her and flick my tongue over her clit.

Eden's knees wobble, but she holds herself up, grips that bar behind her for dear life as I go to town on her lady parts like a starving man at a banquet. She feels so warm, tastes so sweet. She's so responsive to my touch, and as I piston my fingers in and out of her wet heat, I sweep the flat of my tongue over her clit in slow, broad licks, then attack her sensitive little nub and suck it hard. Her legs twitch and quake and the most beautiful noises fall from her open mouth.

When I curl my fingers inside her she releases the bar behind her and grips my hair instead, thrusts her honeyed cunt at my face in obvious command. "Hunter!"

Who am I to disobey?

So I double-down on my thrusting/curling combo, and alternate sucking and licking her swollen clit, willing the elevator to go slower so I can spend more time between her thighs. But then I feel her pussy's telltale quiver and it only takes another second for her to come apart and scream my name.

Her chest heaves with ragged breaths and her legs shake uncontrollably. Her fingers tighten in my hair, twisting, pulling, and her pussy grips my fingers so hard it's making my cock jealous. And just when I think she's done and I'm about to pull away, she thrusts her hips forwards one last time and sweet, molten heat splashes across my tongue and drips down my chin.

Wow. In all my years of eating pussy I've never had that happen before. It's unexpected, but not unwelcome. I stare up at her in awe.

But her cheeks have turned pink and her gaze darts to the side, away from mine. Her smile is gone, replaced with something that looks a lot like regret. "Your beard is wet," she murmurs, tugging at her skirt.

I tighten my grip on her legs and block the descent of her dress. "Baby, what's wrong?"

"Nothing," she says, her tone defensive and her brow pulling down as she tugs at her dress again.

And that's when it hits me. She's not regretful.

She's embarrassed.

Has she never come like that before? A part of me likes the thought. That I'm the only man to experience her full passion that way.

Or is she expecting me to shame her for it?

Your beard is wet.

A rush of anger hits me like a truck as I realise it's the latter. "Eden, look at me." I lever to my feet and cup her face, force her to look at me. She's tries to shake me off but her resistance is token at best. When her eyes do meet mine I see the stain of tears swimming there. I see the loss of her earlier confidence and it makes my blood boil.

Men really are idiots.

Before I can say anything, though, the elevator dings, announcing our arrival at my apartment. Eden quickly tugs her dress back into place and smoothes down her hair. There's no need. We're completely alone. But if it makes her feel more in control, then I won't take that from her. Even if I do immediately miss the sight of her pillowy thighs and the moisture that decorates them, left in the wake of her orgasm.

The doors open and I take her hand, gently tug her out of the elevator and into the foyer. "Would you like the grand tour?"

What the hell am I saying? Why the fuck am I suddenly nervous? I should be dragging this beautiful woman to my bed, stripping her naked and making her come all over my face again.

"Sure," she says, her voice soft, almost shy. Small. It doesn't suit her. "But, may I use the bathroom first?"

"Of course." I indicate the direction of the powder room across from the foyer. "I'll be waiting," I say, hoping she can see the need in my gaze as I lock my eyes to hers.

Eden ducks her head and vanishes into the bathroom just as a text vibrates my phone in my pocket. Finley apparently anticipated my wishes and deleted the security tape. My girl is safe from potential embarrassment. I send a quick reply of thanks, then grin as an idea hits me.

I know exactly how to get tonight back on track.

I open my text chain with Eden and quickly tap out another message, smile as I hear her phone ding with the incoming text, then rush to put my plan into action.

The longest five minutes of my life passes before Eden cautiously pokes her head around the corner of my bedroom door and peers inside.

"Hunter?"

I stand before her, unashamedly naked, my cock gripped in my fist and hard as fuck. "That's *Daddy* to you, Baby Girl."

6

E *den*

Is it possible to die from being over-aroused?

Asking for a friend.

Hunter—*Daddy*—stands before me. Tall and lean and gloriously naked, his body is a feast for my eyes and *damn* am I hungry.

The text I'd received while in the toilet had been more than a little vague.

Daddy: Follow the breadcrumbs.

After I'd washed up and come out of the

bathroom, I'd found his T-shirt on the floor, folded into an arrow and pointing down the hallway. That had led to his jeans, also on the floor, the legs splayed in the direction of the open doorway that led me to his sumptuous bedroom and the manifestation of male perfection waiting by the foot of the bed.

"Hunter?"

"That's *Daddy* to you, Baby Girl."

Yep. I'm pretty sure I'm going to die tonight.

And to think, I'd thought jeans, a T-shirt and no shoes was sexy.

The sight of this man completely naked is more than sexy. Hell, it's doing things to my lady parts that are probably illegal. Definitely indecent.

And I am so here for it.

Dropping my purse on the floor, I move towards him, steady my breathing and moisten my lips. I don't miss the way his eyes lock on to my mouth and the tiny movement of my tongue. The heat of his gaze does much to negate my earlier embarrassment. I still can't believe I splooshed all over his face. In an elevator of all places. Don't get me wrong—it was *amazing*. And if I ever meet the person who taught him how to eat pussy like that, I will shake their hand. But—

"Baby Girl, look at me."

At the sound of Hunter's deep voice, I realise my gaze has drifted away from his, my focus blurring the way it always does when my brain gets snagged on something and over-thinks things.

I give myself a mental shake. I should be ogling this man's sculpted torso and strong neck, not obsessing over my pussy's earlier lack of discretion. I should be stroking my hands over the arm porn that is his biceps, not getting lost in my own head. I spend more than enough time there as it is, alone with my thoughts. And to be completely honest, he doesn't seem at all bothered by what happened in the elevator. I don't think he even noticed when it happened in the back of his car. Which means it's just my insecurities rearing their ugly heads and—

"Eden."

Oh, crap. I've done it again. *Focus.* Stupid brain.

Hunter chuckles and shakes his head, anchors his hands on his hips. "Do I have to have words with your inner monologue? Is that who's stealing your attention away from me?"

My jaws drops. "How did you know?" He's eerily perceptive.

Moving closer, he holds his hands out and beckons me to him. "Because you love books, and I haven't met a single person yet who loves books as much as you do who hasn't had an inner monologue."

I eye him cautiously. "Do you have them?" I've never met another weirdo like me and my heart skips a beat when he smiles and nods.

"I do. Now, come here."

His simple observation quietens my mind. The assurance of his simple command excites it. I take his hands in mine and laugh as he yanks me into his arms, as he wraps me in their strength.

"You're wearing too many clothes, Baby Girl."

In an instant his lips are on mine, firm and demanding. I open up to him, let him devour me as I explore his nakedness with greedy hands. His body is as firm as his kiss, with silky soft skin stretched taut over his muscled frame. I run my fingers lightly down his chest, follow the subtle valley that carves its way between his pecs and the sixpack that covers his abdomen.

His lips curve into a smile as he kisses me, as I slide my hand lower to follow the line of hair that arrows downwards from his navel to his cock and... *gee-zuz*.

Talk about a treasure trail, because I just hit paydirt.

His cock is *huge*.

I mean, sure, I've seen it, and yeah, it has been inside me, so I know he's big, but to feel it against my palm, to know I can't even wrap my fingers fully around it...? *Wow*. I nonetheless try to wrap my hand around it, and his lusty moans tell me he appreciates the effort.

That's when I feel the zipper of my dress descending, feel the latch of my bra come undone, followed by that feeling of blessed relief all women feel when we remove our constraints at the end of the day. Reluctantly, I let go of his cock until he finishes undressing me. He rewards me with a slow, sensual caress, teases me with gentle, fleeting touches as he slips my dress down my body and tugs my bra free from my arms.

And he never once breaks our kiss.

I step out of my heels and then I'm as naked

as he is, with nothing between us to hide my big belly and saggy boobs, and still he's kissing me, exploring me. Tugging me close and pressing all his lean hardness against my multitude of softness. But instead of feeling self-conscious about my size, instead of analysing why a man who looks like Hunter would be getting down and dirty with a woman who looks like me, I make the decision to just go with it.

To stop thinking.

To start feeling.

To simply let myself live in the moment and see where it goes. Consequences be damned.

I reach for him again and slide my palm against the silky steel of his cock.

"*Fuck*. I need to be inside you." The words, his voice, a guttural promise that sends a shiver of pleasure through my entire being, from booty to brain. "But first...."

"Yes?"

Hunter locks his hand around my throat and forces my gaze to meet his. "I want to watch you come again." Reaching between my thighs, he slips two fingers inside me. "You're so wet, baby," he murmurs by my ear. "So tight. So good. My good girl." He thrusts deep and slow, adds his thumb to the mix, pressing firmly against my clit. "I want to watch you fall apart. I want to hear you scream my name."

I close my eyes and lean into the safety of Hunter's grip and I almost don't recognise the sounds coming from deep inside me. The panting, growling, animalistic noises he elicits as he thrusts faster and faster.

"How long will it take to make you come again?"

My legs are shaking, my muscles clenching. My fingers curl, one hand around a bicep, one around his cock, pumping in time to his thrusting. I have to be hurting him, but he doesn't seem to care. Faster and harder he thrusts, the wet sounds coming from between my legs mingling with our panting and moaning, until my breath suddenly sticks in my lungs before dislodging in a primal scream.

I throw my head back. "*Daddy!*"

"That's it, Baby Girl. Come for Daddy. Come for me, my dirty girl."

Looking up at him, I see the lust in his eyes, the pride, and I know his hand is soaked, can feel how slick my thighs are. But this time I don't feel ashamed. This time when Daddy looks at me I don't imagine the revulsion I've always seen in men's eyes. He stares at me like I'm the most wonderful, most beautiful thing he's ever seen.

And I realise that's it.

That's why I'm able to be myself with him, unashamedly wanton and free.

And he told me! When we sat in the back seat of his car and I rambled on and on, he fucking *told* me, but I didn't believe him. Not really.

Hunter *sees* me.

He doesn't scold me or tell me I'm disgusting. When he calls me dirty he says it with affection. With wonder. And when a second orgasm follows closely behind the first and my knees begin to buckle, he's there. He's holding me up and pulling me close, whispering sweet affirmations of lust, kissing my shoulder, my neck, my mouth. Sweeping his tongue between my lips and taking control of me with one hell of a passionate and all-consuming kiss.

When he pulls away, he leans his forehead against mine, chuckles, then sighs softly, contentedly. "Good to know it's not just my tongue that gets that reaction."

I giggle. "You do realise your cock got the

same reaction on the back seat of your car, right?"

His brow pulls down, turns thoughtful. "I can't say that I do. Huh." He cocks one eyebrow and grins. "I guess we'll just have to do it again."

"For science?"

He kisses me again, quick and playful. "Where the fuck have you been all my life?"

I shrug. "Probably somewhere with my nose in a book."

His grin grows feral and he clamps one big hand around my wrist. "Come with me."

7

H*unter*

Eden stumbles as I drag her out of my bedroom and down the hall, so I stop and throw her over my shoulder. She squeals and laughs and tells me to put her down, that she's too heavy.

I don't listen.

I can't put her down. I won't.

My Baby Girl needs to know I can take care of her. Needs to know I couldn't care less how big she is. I'm bigger. I'm taller, stronger.

Her weight means nothing to me.

It's her sharp mind and sharper tongue that have me enthralled.

Her lush body and dripping-wet pussy are just the icing on the cake.

We pass through the foyer and I shove open the door on the other side.

Eden giggles as she jiggles on my shoulder. "Where are you taking me? The bed is back that way."

Once inside the room, I put her on her feet, making sure to block her view with my body. "Close your eyes."

Eden gives me a look that makes me want to fuck her senseless, then huffs a sigh and rolls her eyes before closing them. "Yes, Daddy."

I place a quick kiss on her lips then turn her around, rest my chin on her head and my hands on her hips. "Open your eyes, Baby Girl."

Her breathy gasp is music to my ears. "A library." Pulling away from me, she moves to the books and runs her fingers over the spines, almost reverently. There's thrillers and horrors and romances, cookbooks and law texts and biographies, and a whole section dedicated to erotic art that I can't wait to show her. But it's the law texts that catch Eden's eye. She looks at me over her shoulder. "You're a lawyer?"

"I am," I say, and fold my arms over my chest, lean against the doorframe. "Is that okay?"

Her eyes narrow as she turns to look at me fully, but her voice lacks censure. "Depends. Who do you work for?"

My mouth kicks up at one corner. It's a fair question. I push away from the doorframe and stalk towards her. "I used to work for a firm specialising in corporate law, but now I'm an IP litigator."

"So... you help authors with copyright issues?"

"Authors, artists, musicians. Anyone who needs help with copyright or patent complaints." I reach for her and pull her close, kiss my way from her shoulder to the base of her throat. "Once, I even helped a street magician prove copyright for an illusion his ex copied and claimed she created."

Eden leans into me, slides her hands up my chest. "If you weren't already naked, I'd be ripping your clothes off right about now."

"You'd ruin my best jeans and T-shirt?" I tease.

"Hmm, good point. I'd hate to ruin that sexy ensemble," she teases right back, then shoves me backwards so I stumble and fall onto the sofa. "So how about I do something else to show my appreciation?"

When she grabs a cushion and lowers herself to her knees, my gut tightens with lust and my breathing stutters. "Eden."

"That's *Baby Girl* to you, Daddy."

I can't help myself. I laugh out loud as she throws my earlier words back at me, and I slide my hand into her hair, grip her tight, guide her down as she wraps her pretty pout around my cock and proceeds to give me the best blowjob of my adult life.

It was this exact same sofa I'd sat on when she texted me earlier tonight, when she made my cock hard and a possessive streak I never knew I owned reared its ugly head.

My fists tighten in her hair.

Eden is mine.

Lord knows she's owned me from the first night she texted me. It doesn't matter that it wasn't by design, that she thought I was someone else. I will be forever grateful her date was a douchebag that night, because he'd led her straight to me, and unlike that fucking idiot, I know a good thing when I see it.

From the moment I received Eden's first

text, I have been captivated by her. And tonight, when I saw her standing outside the restaurant, her curious gaze peering in at me, I wanted her. Craved her. Needed her. Needed to feel her lush mouth pressed to mine, needed to explore her soft body and feel it pinned beneath me.

She's so beautiful.

A goddamned goddess.

Her fingernails dig into my thighs just as I feel a tightening at the base of my spine. I'm so fucking close to coming, but I don't want to come in her mouth. I want to feel her pussy clench around me. I want to feel her drip down my hard length and ruin my sofa.

"Baby."

She looks up at me with those gorgeous bedroom eyes and I almost shoot my load, but I manage to control myself long enough to yank her off the floor and pull her onto my lap.

"Condom?" she pants.

"Side table." I point to the small table beside the sofa.

In record time, she has me sheathed and straddled and I'm sinking inside her, her pussy gripping me tight as I thrust up into her. *Fuck.* She feels so good. So hot, so tight, so wet. And I get my wish. She is dripping, soaking me and my furniture with her feminine heat. I fucking love it. She's so open, so free.

So sexy and uninhibited.

The way she rocks her hips, riding me with slow deliberation, is driving me crazy. I want to touch her everywhere, want to explore every inch of her body. Her full breasts sway in front of my face. I yank her closer, wrap my arms around her back and hold her to me as I take one rosy nipple between my teeth and gently tug.

She moans softly. "Daddy."

I'm a bossy man—always have been—and I love being in control, but I don't consider myself to be dominant. I'm not into pain or discipline or any of that stuff, but I think taking care of Eden might just be my new kink.

Maybe being her Daddy all the time is something she'd be open to. Maybe after I make her come, after I hear her scream and watch her face morph in ecstasy, I'll bathe her, feed her, ask her to stay the night. I'll take care of her. Show her how she should be treated all the time. How she should *expect* to be treated.

Eden whimpers as she grinds down on me, as she rocks her hips with more urgency. I release her nipple and lick a path up her throat, kiss the corner of her mouth. "You going to be a good girl and come for Daddy?"

She sinks her teeth into her bottom lip and nods, so I sink my fingers into her fleshy hips and help her achieve her goal.

It's what any good daddy would do.

I move my body in time with hers, meet each roll of her hips by thrusting up into her, bottoming out inside her. The feeling is exquisite.

My breathing grows heavy and the tightening in my spine returns. I'm so fucking close.

Eden tightens her grip on me, her fingernails scoring the flesh across the back of my shoulders. Releasing her bottom lip from the steel trap of her teeth, her mouth forms that perfect little O I've been waiting for, and the sound of her impending orgasm blends with the wet slapping coming from between our thighs.

Like a symphony of sex.

Her eyes are shut tight, her head tilted back, and her whole body jiggles as she bounces on my cock. I want her to come with me. Want to fall over the edge of that glorious abyss together. Want to hear our voices mingle in mutual pleasure as she rides me into next week.

Reaching between us, I stroke my thumb over her clit, apply just enough pressure to trigger the response I want. The response I crave.

Eden is coming.

Her movements lose their rhythm, grow more erratic as she starts to scream. Her fingers dig into my back and she throws her head forwards, bites my shoulder. Hard. My own grip on her body tightens, pulling her down as I continue thrusting up, filling her with my cock. Pounding into her, surrounded by the smell of leather-bound books and the musk of sex.

And then there we are. Both crying out for the other. Both coming at the same time. Panting and cursing and clinging to one another as though our very lives depend on it. Falling head first into an erotic abyss.

Maybe even falling... *in love*?

8

E *den*

When our orgasms subside, we rest for a moment, then Hunter excuses himself to dispose of the condom and I'm left standing, awkwardly witnessing the mess we made on his expensive-looking leather sofa.

I should be embarrassed but, weirdly, I'm not. Maybe because the sex high is still lingering in my brain. Or maybe because Hunter seems to enjoy the fact my body responds this way to sex. Either way, when he returns and slips his arms around me, I feel things I haven't felt in the presence of a man in a very long time.

Content.

Safe.

Cared for.

I wrap my arms around his middle, settle my head against his chest and breathe him in. I know this whole night has been nuts, and I really need to text my friend again and let her know I'm okay. That not only is Hunter not a serial killer, he's quite possibly the nicest man I've ever met, we've just had the best sex of my life, and that I do not want this night to end.

But it will end.

Fairytales always do.

Still, if I can stretch it out a little further....

"Hunter?"

"Mmm?"

"Sooo... when do I get that grand tour?"

His body shakes with laughter and it vibrates through me. It's a good feeling. "You saying you haven't seen enough?"

I tilt my head back and stare up at him, smile at him and the cheeky grin he's throwing my way, reflecting my own good mood. "Don't get me wrong, the bedroom was great, and the library is amazing," I say, and lightly tug at his beard. "But...."

He grabs my hand and kisses my fingers, then cocks one brow with mock severity. "But?"

"Would it be asking too much for a tour of the kitchen?"

His grin returns. "You hungry, baby?"

"After that workout? Famished."

He chuckles again and my heart skips a beat, and I realise he's staring down at me with a wealth of warmth and affection shining in his clear blue eyes. Stroking back my sweat-slicked hair, he says, "What kind of Daddy would I be if I let my Baby Girl starve? Especially since you haven't had a decent meal tonight."

My cheeks heat, his tender touch scorching right down to the heart of me. But my banter knows no bounds. Even without sexting, this is how I flirt. "I know, right? A girl cannot live on salad alone."

"And who eats salad without steak anyway?"

"Or bacon?"

"Or potatoes drowned in butter?"

I giggle as Hunter repeats the food rant I'd texted at him while hiding in the restaurant bathroom, but then my insecurities snap to and take over and I drop my gaze, break the connection we had and chew at my bottom lip as I debate my next words, my next move.

But Daddy is perceptive. He lifts my hand to his mouth, kisses my fingers again. "Don't hide from me, baby. Talk to me."

Cautiously, I lift my gaze to his, then flick it away again. His stare is intense. "Would it be ridiculous to think.... Would it be possible to...." I take a breath, find my courage and meet his gaze. "Can I see you again?" Before he can answer, I push on, my discomfort clear as my words spill out of me. "I get it if this was just a one-night thing for you, and I know I'm not the type of woman most men want to date. You wouldn't be the first man to tell he doesn't have room in his life for a woman who takes up so much space," I tell him, my mouth twisting to one side. "I've had a lot of fun tonight and I've enjoyed your company in real life even more than I did when we were just texting, and not just for the sex, although that was spectacular. But I really enjoyed...."

How do I say this?

"Being taken care of?"

Yep. See? Perceptive.

I nod and watch his face, watch for the

tiniest change in his expression. "Yes. Is that wrong?"

His smile is slow and broad, causing his eyes to crinkle at the corners. "Is it wrong that I enjoyed taking care of you? That I want to take care of you more?"

"You do?"

"Hm-mm. Starting with a shower and followed by a late dinner. And if you agree to stay the night, I'll take you out for brunch in the morning. There's a café down the street that makes the best *pain au chocolat* you'll ever eat."

I can't help myself. I have to push this new boundary. "And if I don't want to stay the night?"

His smile softens into a smirk. He knows what I'm doing. "Then I'll have Finley drive you home. Of course, he'd just have to pick you up again in the morning for brunch, so...."

"So, I should stay the night."

"Exactly."

"For Finley's sake?"

He kisses my forehead. "It would be the considerate thing to do."

I snuggle against the big man again, sigh contentedly as he strokes my hair. "I suppose I could stay," I tell him. "If it means being pampered by my Daddy."

Hunter chuckles and the soothing sound of it surrounds me as surely as his arms. Holds me firmly in place, right where he wants me.

Right where I want to be.

"Daddy?"

"Yes, Baby Girl?"

I rest my chin on his chest. "I'm really glad I drunk-texted you that night."

"I'm really glad your date was an arse."

I turn my head and glance at the sofa. "And I'm sorry I ruined your furniture."

"I'm not." Lifting me off my feet, he kisses me soundly. "Now, let's get you cleaned up, fed, and ready for bed, okay, Baby Girl?"

My smile is quick, and my heart is full as I answer him. "Yes, Daddy."

EPILOGUE

One year later

Hunter

I straighten my tie one last time as the music swells, announcing the arrival of my soon-to-be wife.

Eden, my sweet Baby Girl, agreed to marry me after only four months of dating. I would have been happy to elope then and there, but she insisted we do it right, that we wait a little longer and make sure—*really* sure—that our

Daddy/Baby Girl dynamic wasn't just a phase that would wane in time.

One year in, and if anything, our kinky bond has only gotten stronger. I love taking care of her in any and every way she needs. It fills a void in me I hadn't realised I had until she came into my life, one properly punctuated text at a time.

I love Eden more than I can ever put into words, and as I watch her walk towards me in a pale pink confection of a dress, carrying a bouquet of paper flowers, the petals crafted from discarded books, I want to take her in my arms, lift that voluminous skirt above her waist and shove my face between her pretty thighs. I want to feel their warmth and pillowy softness squeeze around my head as I make her scream and drink her passion....

But they tend to frown on such things in public libraries. Because that's where my Baby Girl wanted to get married, surrounded by her beloved books. So I content myself with imagining her sexy voice begging for my cock, and I beam at her as she stops beside me, a knowing look on her face as she observes my wicked grin.

"Daddy," she whispers by way of greeting,

her perfect pout curling around the word in a way that makes my hard-as-rock cock flex against the front of my trousers, desperate to be free and buried inside my woman. Something she is all too aware of, if her quick glance down my body is any indication.

Leaning down, I press a kiss to her cheek, then whisper, "It's all for you, Baby Girl."

She giggles, and for a moment I think she might kiss me, but then a throat clears behind us—Finley, acting as witness for our nuptials —and the celebrant standing before us begins to speak.

The ceremony is brief and to the point. There are no songs about love, or famous quotes about marriage, just an 'I do' from each of us and a promise to love each other no matter what life throws at us. And as I slip a golden ring on Eden's finger, I notice she isn't even looking at it. She's watching me. Smiling up at me. Staring at me with so much heat in her gaze that I feel it all the way to my soul.

She burns me alive and I love every fucking second I'm in that fire.

When the celebrant announces us as husband and wife, Eden grabs my hand and practically drags me away, leading me through the labyrinth of bookshelves until we come to her office.

"And what exactly are we doing in here?" I ask, grinning as she locks the door behind us.

She slides her hands down my chest until they rest on my belt buckle. "You're going to do me."

Ah, my sweet Eden. My perfectly dirty girl. "What if someone hears us?"

Her sweet smile turns wicked and her nimble fingers make short work of my belt and zipper. "Then I guess you should put something in my mouth."

I fist my hand in her hair, ruining the fancy hairstyle she'd worn for the ceremony, and force her to her knees. "Take me deep, Baby Girl. Take my cock to the back of your throat."

Over the past year, I've learned a lot about my woman. The way she takes her coffee, the cute little snort she makes when she laughs too hard, how she loves to bake chocolate chip cookies when she's in a good mood, or how she needs some space, a comfy blanket and a good book when she's in a bad one. And I've learned how much she loves my cock.

Riding it. Fucking it. Sucking it.

I have never met a woman who loves giving

head as much as Eden. She is truly the perfect woman. My perfect match.

My soulmate.

But it's not just the sex. It's everything. It's the way she takes care of me when I'm pulling an all-nighter for a case, bringing me food and endless cups of coffee, keeping me company until she inevitably falls asleep on the sofa, and I carry her to bed. It's the way she dances around the kitchen in the morning as she makes us breakfast. It's the songs she sings in the shower, and the way she perches her reading glasses on the end of her nose and glances over the top of them in what she calls her 'Cranky Librarian' look. 'Sexy As Fuck Librarian' would be more accurate.

It's the books she recommends because she thinks I would like them, and I usually do. It's the kindness she shows others, the sounds she makes when she eats something delicious, and the text messages we still share. The good mornings, and the honey-do lists, conversations about our plans for the weekend, or which restaurant to try for lunch next week, or the everyday argument about what to eat for dinner, which generally turns into flirty sexting, and more than once has ended with me tracking her down and eating her pussy.

But mostly, it's the way she comes to me when she needs comfort, the way she curls up in my lap when she comes home from work, snuggling into me for a few precious moments to decompress at the end of her day. The way she makes me feel as if I'm the only person on the planet who can soothe her anxious mind and put her world to rights.

It's my favourite time of day, and I'd be lying if I said it wasn't a power trip, but it's a power I wield with care. And as I stare down at my wife on her knees, taking my cock down her throat like the good girl she is, I know I'm not the one with the *real* power.

That's all her.

Easing her off my cock, I haul her to her feet, walk her backwards until her arse hits the desk and lift her skirt out of my way, chuckling as I reveal her naked pussy.

"Good girl," I murmur, then groan as I slide my full length inside her tight, wet passage. "Fuck, Baby Girl. I will never grow tired of this feeling."

She clings to my suit clad shoulders, bunching the fabric in her fists, her eyes half shut, her mouth forming the perfect little O I adore as her breath stutters out of her. "Which feeling is that?"

I thrust deeper. "That you own me, baby." I thrust harder. "Body, mind." I hold her tighter. "Heart."

The word barely leaves my mouth when her body begins to shake with her impending orgasm. Her thighs quiver and her cunt tightens. She is so wet. I pull out of her and fall to my knees, clasping my lips over her clit, then lapping at her sweetness as she screams for me. As she gushes for me. I will never tire of that either.

Levering to my feet, I pull her into my arms and hold her tightly, revelling in the way she sags against my chest until her breathing evens out.

"You didn't come," she murmurs.

I grin against her now messy hair, then pull back and stare at her, one brow cocked and my voice stern. "Oh, I'm sorry. Did you think we were finished?"

A blush stains her cheeks and her throat visibly bobs. "No, Daddy."

"Good, because we've only just started." I fist my cock and feed it to her greedy pussy, groan at the feel of her slick heat surrounding me, of my thick length stretching her open. Then I pound into her hard and fast, her wedding dress bunched up between us, her fingernails digging into my arse, her desk banging against the wall behind us with the force of our fucking.

"Oh, fuck." She moans, and I know she's close to coming again. Then she bites her lip and her body tightens, her pussy clamping down on me so damn tight that I follow her right over the edge and into that blessed abyss.

"I love you, Baby Girl," I whisper by her ear, then bury my face in the crook of her neck to catch my breath.

"I love you too, Daddy."

The smile that spreads across my face, the joy I feel deep in my soul every time she says those words, still blows my mind. And to think, it all started with a drunken text to a wrong number. My number.

> Baby Girl: You, sir, are an addlepated twit with the manners of a drunken goat, and less academic acumen than my left arse cheek!

It still makes me chuckle, so much so that I had it framed and hung in my office. It's a great conversation starter. And replying to that late night tongue-lashing is still the best decision I have ever made. Because it led me to Eden.

My sweet, passionate wife.

My Baby Girl.

The love of my life.

The End

Turn the page...

Good girl.

Turn the page again to read the
text that started it all...

THE TEXT
THAT
Started
IT ALL...

LATE ONE NIGHT...

My brow lifts and I can't help the laugh that escapes me as I re-read the text that just hit my phone. I rack my sleep deprived brain, searching for the name of anyone who could have sent me such a text at three in the morning, but come up short. I may be a lawyer, sure, but last I checked, no one was even slightly annoyed with me, let alone angry enough to call me an addlepated twit.

And who in the world even uses words like addlepated and twit anymore?

Obviously I'm not the intended target of this rant, so with another laugh and a shake of my head, I mute my notifications, put the phone face down on my bedside table, and go back to reading my book.

But it doesn't end there.

Five minutes later, my gaze slides sideways, distracted by my phone vibrating as another text comes through. Turning the page of my book, I try to ignore the light coming from the underside of my phone, alerting me to the unread message. I read a few more lines when it buzzes again, lights up again, and I find myself intrigued, wondering what insults my mystery messenger has concocted this time.

Putting aside my book, I pick up the phone, swipe it to life and open my messages app.

Yep. It's them, and they're still pissed off.

Unknown number: How you can call yourself an intellectual and say libraries are obsolete in the same breath continues to baffle me.

Unknown number: And before you again call me "just a librarian", I think we both know what you meant to say was just a woman, as I highly doubt you would have had the temerity to say such utter bullshit to another man.

Unknown number: And the fact you thought I would still want to fuck your parsimonious arse after your appalling display of ignorance, coupled with your backhanded compliments about my physical appearance, only further shows your true character, or lack there of.

Unknown number: And just in case I didn't make it clear, it takes more than paying for dinner in a cheap hotel restaurant to get into my oversized panties. Arsehole.

Holy shit.

The more I read, the more my jaw drops. This woman definitely has the wrong number, but I am so here for it. If I had to guess, I'd say she went on a first date and it did not go well.

Not surprising. In my experience most men are idiots, especially when confronted with a intelligent woman who knows her worth and isn't afraid to flaunt it.

And from what she has said so far, the guy was a conceited twat. I mean, come on. It takes a special kind of moron to learn their date is a librarian and then tell them libraries are obsolete.

How do men like this even get dates in the first place? Seriously. I want to know. How? Is it a numbers game, or is he just *really* good looking?

Maybe... I should ask her.

She's obviously awake. And it would be rude not to respond, right?

It takes me all of three seconds to make up my mind and type out a reply.

> Me: Hello. I just wanted to let you know you have the wrong number, but please feel free to continue venting. I am wide awake and willing to listen, because honestly, you sound far more interesting than the book I'm reading.

While I wait to see if she responds, I add her number to my contact list.

Mystery Girl.

Mystery Girl: Oh, so you're pretending to read books now? As opposed to your much preferred "journals".

Mystery Girl: An elitist academic twat such as yourself would know a good book if it smacked you in the face. Dare I ask what "book" you're reading?

Is it weird that I feel giddy? I'm a fifty-three year old man. *Giddy* should not be a part of the job description. And yet, as I respond to my mystery girl's scathing text, that's exactly how I feel.

Me: Moby Dick.

Mystery Girl: Moby Dick? Seriously?

Me: Yes. By Herman Melville.

> Mystery Girl: I know who wrote Moby Dick, thank you very much. I'm just surprised that you do.

More dots appear and I grin as I wait with bated breath for her next accusation.

> Mystery Girl: Seriously, is this a joke? Are you messing with me right now?

> Me: Not messing with you. Not a joke. Very serious. And very, very bored.

My heart skips a little as the dots reappear.

> Mystery Girl: Uh-huh. You almost had me. Moby Dick. For a moment there I forgot the internet exists.

> Me: What does that mean?

> Mystery Girl: Like you don't know what that means. Like you didn't just Google "The top 100 most pretentious classics of all time". Please. Don't try to weasel your way out of a tongue-lashing by pretending you're not you.

> Me: Sweetheart, I would kill to
> lashed by your quick tongue,
> and I promise I'm not trying to
> weasel out of anything. You
> really do have the wrong number,
> but as I stated before, I am
> happy to be your sounding
> board. I'd hate for such an
> elegant rant to vanish into the
> void unread and
> unacknowledged. You have a
> way with words that would make
> any man of worth sit up and pay
> attention.

It's not a lie.

Hands down, no doubt about it, you give me a woman with a sharp mind and a sharper tongue and I am like putty in her hands.

Because I would love to go out with a woman like this. Hell, her vocabulary alone has me needing to know everything about her.

And... *fuck.* I have a hunch she could whisper the word temerity in my ear and I'd come like an untried teen. And let's just say it has not gone unnoticed that she does not abbreviate anything. No acronyms, no emojis. Just full sentences and proper punctuation.

People these days have no idea how sexy

that is. And I know, okay. Getting a hard-on over correct grammar is a very particular kink but it's mine and I own it so... shut up.

Little dots flicker on my screen, disappearing and reappearing again, as if she's second guessing her reply. Or my sincerity. Probably both.

> Mystery Girl: Are you drunk?

My laughter barks out of me. She does not disappoint.

> Me: No. Are you?

> Mystery Girl: Very! But that doesn't mean I'm not capable of critical thinking. You can't gaslight your way out of this one, Corey.

> Me: No gaslighting. Only truth.

> Me: I promise.

> Me: Also, not Corey. You really do have the wrong number, and I really am reading the World's most boring book.

Several minutes pass without a response, but just as I begin to think she must have fallen asleep, the little dots reappear on my screen. They blink away for what feels like forever. She's either writing an essay, or wording her next insult very carefully, and I can't decide which one I would prefer to see.

Finally I hear the ding I've been waiting for.

> Mystery Girl: Say, for the sake of argument, that I believe you, and you are in fact not Corey. Tell me, in ten words or less, your thoughts on libraries and their role in modern society.

My grin stretches wide and I rub my hands together. Ten words? She's being generous. I can do it in five.

> Me: Libraries separate man from animal.

> Mystery Girl: And where do you stand on women who don't fit into societal norms. Plus-sized women in particular?

Scrolling back through her earlier messages, I am reminded of what she wrote about backhanded compliments regarding her appearance and her oversized panties. My brain conjures up a litany of insults her idiot date could have levelled at her and my blood boils.

> Me: Stand? I would kneel at her feet.

And eat her pussy until she screamed my name.

> Mystery Girl: Really? Because that wasn't the vibe I got earlier tonight when you said you only date fat chicks because they try harder in bed.

My jaw ticks and my skin feels tight and I want to find this Corey prick and smash my fist into his face. But before I can convey any of this to my Mystery Girl, another texts flashes to life on my phone.

> Mystery Girl: I suggest you try harder at not being a complete and utter cunt. Good night and good riddance.

I'm chuckling again. I can't help it. The woman is funny. Yes, it sucks that she had a horrible interaction with a member of my sex and for that I am sorry, but her quick mind and sharp tongue have me craving something I've neither wanted nor needed in a bloody long time.

Genuine connection with another person.

With a woman.

I scroll through our conversation one more time before putting my phone and book away and flicking off the light beside my bed. I can't say I'm not disappointed by the outcome of our exchange, but I suppose it's not surprising after the night she had.

Closing my eyes, an image of a beautiful, voluptuous woman forms in my mind, and try as I might to ignore the erection tenting my sheets, I can't.

I don't want to.

Fisting my cock, I imagine my girl's voice, one that is both sultry and sweet, whispering words like 'temerity' and 'cunt' and 'addlepated'.

And I come so fast it makes my head spin.

Sleep comes swiftly after and I dream of

her, my mystery girl. I dream of soft curves, sassy word play, and sexy oversized panties.

The next afternoon, I find myself scrolling through my conversation with Mystery Girl, wondering if I should try reaching out to her, when a flurry of messages appears, one after another.

> Mystery Girl: Dear Not Corey, I am so very sorry for messaging you at such an un-godly hour and ranting at you like the harpy I obviously am. I expect you will have blocked me by now, but just in case you haven't, I wanted to apologise for acting like such a cow. I will now lose your number and never bother you again.

> Mystery Girl: I'm really sorry I called you a cunt.

> Mystery Girl: And Moby Dick is garbage. Stop torturing yourself and donate it to your local book fair.

> Mystery Girl: And thank you for what you said about libraries.

> Mystery Girl: And fat chicks.

Mystery Girl: Okay. I'm done now. You'll never hear from me again. Sorry. Again. Have a nice life. Good-bye.

Me: Don't you dare lose my number!

Me: And there's no need to apologise. I know your colourful language wasn't aimed at me. I'm only sorry you had to go through what was obviously a disaster of a first date. You should go out with men more on your level. Not complete morons who don't value every single thing you have to offer.

Like me, I want to add. *You should date me!* But something holds me back. I'd like to think it's gentlemanly instinct, but in truth, I'm a little bit scared. Not of dating an intelligent woman, never that. But it's been a while since I put myself out there. I'm not sure I even know how to flirt anymore.

Me: Would it be okay if we kept talking?

Those little dots appear...

> Mystery Girl: I would like that.

So would I. Very, *very* much.

Two weeks later...

> Mystery Girl: What are you wearing?

Fuck. Yes.
Here we go...

Thank you for reading my little book.
I hope you enjoyed Hunter and Eden's story.

MORE FROM JENNIE KEW

THE Q COLLECTION

No Rest For The Wicked

I Saw, I Conquered, I Came

Pushing Rope

Dirty Laundry

Santa Claus Is Coming

Carved In Stone

Battery Operated Boyfriend

Tying The Knot

Quirky: The Complete Q Collection

ACKNOWLEDGEMENTS

To my family for all their encouragement, their love and understanding, thank you for being you and for putting up with me being me, especially when deadlines are involved.

And to my readers, thank you for taking this journey with me, and for allowing me to share with you all the people and places who occupy my head and my heart. I hope you enjoy reading about them as much as I enjoy writing about them.

MEET THE AUTHOR

Jennie has always enjoyed reading but never had aspirations of becoming a published author. At least not until a dance with death made her ask herself what she really wanted out of life, and she's been writing ever since.

When not writing stories about her imaginary friends, Jennie can usually be found reading a book, watching a movie or building stuff out of Lego. She lives in regional New South Wales with her husband, her husband's magnificent beard, and their small menagerie of furry companions.

www.jenniekew.com

www.ingramcontent.com/pod-product-compliance
Lightning Source LLC
Chambersburg PA
CBHW050759080726
47590CB00021B/3136